# A Pony in Need

CHARMING PONIES

# A Pony in Need

LOIS SZYMANSKI

HarperFestival®
*A Division of* HarperCollins*Publishers*

Charming Ponies: A Pony in Need
Copyright © 1995 by Lois Knight Szymanski
Printed in the United States of America.
www.harpercollinschildrens.com
Library of Congress catalog card number: 96-96266
ISBN 978-0-06-128873-9
Typography by Sasha Illingworth
❖
First published as *Little Icicle* in 1995.

This book, based on a true story, is dedicated
to my husband, Dan, for taking me to Chincoteague
and Assateague each time the yearning comes,
and for fulfilling my dreams.

# A Pony in Need

# *one*

att and Holly pedaled down the black-top trail slowly. Holly's long blonde hair was whisked from her face by the icy breeze. Matt's camera hung from his neck. He was ready to shoot a picture should they see a fox, a rare bird or wild ponies. They passed a group of three women with binoculars around their necks, strolling on the path. Assateague was a haven for birdwatchers, even in the dead of winter.

Matt skirted a frozen patch in the middle of the road. "Let's take the pony trail," he suggested.

Holly nodded, a grin spreading slowly across her face. She knew why Matt wanted to take that trail. He was always looking for the wild ponies that lived on the island. A little earlier they had seen two firemen from the Chincoteague Volunteer Fire Department take this trail. The men had driven by in a pickup truck with a trailer hooked behind. Matt and Holly knew why the firemen were here on the island. When the weather got cold and the grass dried up, they helped the ponies by dropping bales of hay. This year the firemen had started leaving hay for the wild ponies early in December. Now that it was January, it was even colder and there was little grass left to eat. Wherever hay was dropped, ponies would show up.

Matt pedaled faster, the cold wind blowing through his jacket like a blast from the deep freeze. He pulled his green cap down tightly over his ears.

The wind had already made his ears almost as red as his hair, and that was red!

Holly and Matt rode side by side for awhile. Soon they caught up with the hay truck. "Hi, Mr. Donald!" Matt shouted, waving his hand wildly.

"You're going to wreck if you don't watch out," Holly warned Matt. Then she called out, too. "Hi, Mr. Donald! Hi, Mr. Acey!"

The firemen were dragging bales of hay from the back of the trailer. Mr. Donald was a big man with snow white hair. He busted the bales apart while Mr. Acey spread them in a circle for the ponies to find.

Matt and Holly pulled up on their bikes.

"Hi, kids!" Mr. Donald said with a smile. "What brings you out on a cold day like this?"

Holly combed her fingers through her tangled blonde hair. "We got tired of staying in."

"We thought maybe we'd get to see the ponies, too," Matt added. "We haven't seen them in quite a while."

"They'll be moseying up pretty shortly," Mr.

Acey said. "Seems they always know when we bring a new load of hay."

Mr. Donald finished spreading the hay. Then he backed his big red quarter horse out of the trailer. "Get Jeb out," he told Mr. Acey. "We ought to make a round before we go."

A neigh came from inside the trailer. It seemed Jeb agreed!

Matt knew Mr. Donald's horse, Red, but he had never seen Mr. Acey's horse before. He waited as the thin man backed Jeb out of the trailer.

"He looks like Patches, doesn't he?" Mr. Acey grinned as he held his brown-and-white pinto by the reins. Jeb pawed impatiently at the pine needles, his hooves scraping a bare spot on the ground.

"Sure does!" Matt said breathlessly. The big pinto did look like his own patchy colt!

Matt stepped forward to stroke the pinto's neck. The pinto lowered his head. A moment later Mr. Donald and Mr. Acey had swung into their saddles.

"We'll talk to you kids later," Mr. Donald said.

"We have to go check on the ponies."

Holly got off her bike. "Should we wait for the ponies to come?" she asked.

"Yeah, I guess." Matt laid his bike down and kicked through the hay. All of a sudden he felt scratchy hay hit him in the neck. Holly giggled. Then she picked up another handful of hay and threw it high in the air. It came down on top of both of them. Matt picked up an armful and threw it at his friend. Then they were tumbling in the hay, shrieking with laughter!

Holly rolled to one side, then stopped, staring up. Puffs of gray clouds raced by in a darkened sky.

"Look, Matt. It might snow," she said.

Matt rolled over onto his back and stared up, too. "Maybe, but it never sticks to the ground around here."

"Do you think we should head home?" Holly asked.

"No. Let's wait for the ponies." Matt thought a moment, throwing another handful of hay up into the air. "Let's go look for them instead," he suggested.

Holly stood, brushing the hay from her clothes. She grabbed her bike handles and pushed out onto the road again. "Okay. Let's go."

They headed off in the opposite direction from the firemen. Soon they set their bicycles down and walked along the winding path that led to a freshwater pond where the ponies went to drink. Matt knew about the pond from his days of following his pony, Patches, around the island when the pony was just a wild colt.

"Look! Pony tracks!" Holly said.

"These are new," Matt said. "There's no frost on the hoof prints yet. That means ponies were here not long ago." He hurried toward the pond. Then he saw it. Just ahead, a black-and-white pinto was lying on its side. Its back legs were in the pond, frozen all the way up to its hips! The pinto's front legs were stretched out in front of it and it was as still as death.

"Oh, no!" Matt said. Holly followed his eyes. When she saw the pinto, she let out a frightened cry. The two friends sprinted forward, reaching it together.

Matt's hands ran down the pinto's cold, stiff neck. Its eyes were closed. A black-and-white forelock spilled over its forehead, brushing against the closed lids.

Holly laid her head on the pony's stomach. "I can't hear a heartbeat," she whispered.

"I don't feel one either."

"Is it alive?"

"I . . . I don't know. Matt could feel the tears forming behind his eyes. He blinked hard, to push them back. "One of us has to go for help," he said.

Holly looked down at the pony. "One of us should find Mr. Acey and Mr. Donald."

"You're the fastest," Matt said.

"Okay. I'll go." Holly stood. She looked at the pony one more time, her heart sinking. Then she sprinted off, down the trail.

Matt watched her go. He lay his cheek against the pinto's neck, running his hands up and down, trying to rub away the cold. Then he found a stick and poked at the ice around its legs until some broke. Still it didn't move. The pinto's eyelids remained tightly shut. Matt wondered if it could feel his touch or hear his voice as he began to mumble. As he prayed, snowflakes began to swirl down, lying on his cheek, his nose and on the closed eyes of the pinto.

# *two*

**H**olly ran down the path as fast as her sneakered feet would carry her. At the bottom of the hill the path spilled out onto the blacktop trail where they had dropped the bikes. She jerked her bike up from the ground, mounted and pedaled away in one motion. Holly pumped the pedals hard, speeding down the trail, past the hay where she and Matt had played and on toward the place she had last seen the two firemen.

As Holly rounded the bend she could see them riding toward her in the distance, Mr. Donald on the big red mare and Mr. Acey on the shorter pinto. She slowed slightly so she could wave without losing her balance. "Help! Help!" she yelled.

The firemen waved back.

"Come quick!" Holly yelled. Her lungs were bursting from all the running and pedaling. She was sweaty and scared, but she forced out another yell, even louder. "Hurry! We need help. A pony is down!"

The firemen kicked their horses into a trot. Holly stopped, standing with her bike until they reached her.

"What's going on?" Mr. Donald asked gently. "You're as red as a beet. And where is Matt?"

"He's with the pony!" Holly took a deep breath, then continued. "We found a black-and-white pony. It's stuck in the frozen pond." She lowered her voice. "It might even be dead."

"Show us!" Mr. Acey said quickly.

Holly started to pedal away, but Mr. Donald stopped her. "Leave your bike and come here," he commanded.

Holly laid her bike on the edge of the trail and went to stand beside the big red horse. Mr. Donald reached down and grabbed her under the arm. With a powerful tug he pulled her up in front of him. "No sense in pedaling when you can ride a horse," he said. "Now where is this pony?"

Holly grabbed a handful of red mane, squeezed her legs against the saddle and clung tightly. "Take the path that goes to the freshwater pond."

Matt waited patiently. Kneeling on the ground, he pulled the pinto's head onto his lap. The ice he had broken around its legs had become a soupy green slush that wrapped itself around the pony's legs again. Matt stroked the star on its forehead, twisting the forelock gently around his fingers. His heart beat wildly as he counted off the minutes.

It seemed like forever until he heard the snap of brush and the sound of voices coming closer. "Down here!" He called out.

Red came out of the bushes first, followed by Jeb. Mr. Donald lowered Holly to the ground, then dismounted. Mr. Acey was already on his knees with his head on the pony's chest, listening. "It's a mare," he announced.

Mr. Donald placed his hand on her neck and rubbed it gently. "She's icy," he said.

"Icy," Matt repeated thoughtfully. Already he was naming her.

"I think we're too late," Mr. Acey said.

"Well, let's get her out of here anyway and give her a proper burial."

Each of the firemen grabbed the pony from under a front leg. Together they pulled, until the ice cracked free and the pony was up on the bank. Without thinking, Holly pulled her jacket off and began rubbing the pony's back legs furiously. Matt watched her. Then he removed his jacket, too, and began to rub an icy leg.

Mr. Donald started to speak, but Mr. Acey laid a hand on his arm. "Let's get some kind of a pulley rigged up," he suggested.

The men tramped off, through the brush, returning with two long branches. Taking some rope from his saddle, Mr. Donald roped the sticks to it so that Red was dragging them behind. Then the two men roped the pony mare to the branches.

"Matt, do you think you could lead Jeb out of here for me?" Mr. Acey asked.

Matt nodded and took Jeb's bridle. Then Mr. Donald led Red out of the woods onto the trail. Mr. Acey walked beside the mare, steadying her on the makeshift drag as Red pulled her away from the pond.

"Don't get too upset," Mr. Acey said kindly to Matt and Holly. "These things happen."

Matt followed behind, feeling numb all over. He had hoped the pony would be alive. It was quiet as they walked out of the forest. Neither Matt nor Holly felt like talking.

It wasn't until Red had stopped in front of the trailer that anyone spoke again. Then Mr. Acey reached down to untie her. The knot had tightened on the walk out, so he knelt to pick at it.

Mr. Acey's hand jerked up. He stopped picking the knot and put his head on the mare's stomach. "She's breathing!" he shouted. "This mare isn't dead! She's breathing!"

Mr. Donald dropped Red's reins and hurried to feel the mare's neck. "By golly, she is! The walk must have warmed her up! She's got a heartbeat, too!"

Holly grabbed Matt's arm and squeezed. Matt grinned at her.

"Load her up anyway," Mr. Donald said.

"Let's get her to the firehouse and call a vet to check her out from there."

"Come on, kids. You two can ride back to Chincoteague with us. You've had enough trouble today."

"Our bikes—" Matt began.

"We won't leave your bikes," Mr. Acey said. He

lifted Matt's bike up and put it in the back of the pickup truck.

Matt ran to get Holly's bike. They were getting a ride home. But even more important, Icy was getting a ride home, too!

# *three*

Matt and Holly rode in the front of the pickup truck, squashed between the two firemen in the cab. It was just a short ride across the bridge to Chincoteague. Matt stared straight ahead through the glass while the two firemen talked about the snow that was swirling down and whether or not the vet would be in. He glanced over at Holly. She was staring straight ahead, too.

She seemed lost in thoughts of her own.

The pickup truck rolled to a stop in front of the firehouse. Mr. Donald hurried to the back of the trailer. By the time Matt had scrambled out of the front seat, the fireman had already lowered the ramp and was inside, kneeling beside the mare.

"She's still alive," Mr. Donald called. "Let's get her inside."

While Matt and Holly watched, the men carried the pinto into the firehouse.

"Think you two could wrestle a bale of hay out of the trailer for me?" Mr. Donald asked.

Matt nodded and hurried out to the trailer behind Holly. Together, they dragged a bale down the ramp and into the firehouse. After Mr. Acey had cut the bailer twine on the bale, they pulled it apart, spreading the hay in the corner of the firehouse around the mare.

"Wish we had some straw," Mr. Donald said. "But at least we have the hay. It'll have to do."

"I have some straw at home," Matt volunteered.

"Thanks, son," Mr. Donald replied, "but we

aren't even sure she's going to make it yet. The hay will be all right."

Matt looked up at the big clock on the firehouse wall. It was almost five o'clock.

His mother would be starting to worry. As if she were reading his thoughts, Holly touched his arm. "I have to be getting home," she said.

"Me too." Matt knelt down beside the mare. He could hear Mr. Acey talking to the vet on the telephone that hung from the firehouse wall. He touched the mare's face. Feeling the lump of his camera bumping against his chest, he pulled it up, looked through the viewfinder and snapped a picture of the mare. Then he lowered the camera, too sad to shoot again. It seemed almost disrespectful to take her picture when she was like this.

He touched the mare's face again. "Icy," he whispered. "You're going to be okay."

Holly was on her knees beside him. "What did you call her?"

"Icy," Matt answered. "It's her name."

"How do you know?"

"Just do," he replied gruffly.

Holly traced the pinto's nostrils with a finger. As she leaned closer, her long blonde hair brushed Icy's face. "Icy," she repeated. "Open your eyes, Icy. You have to live." As she rubbed the muzzle softly, Matt stroked Icy's neck. As if she knew they were leaving, the mare's eyelids fluttered open. She rolled her eyes a moment, and the air burst through her nostrils fearfully. But as she watched the two and felt their soothing touch, she relaxed, her long dark lashes blinked and her eyes closed again.

"She opened her eyes!" Matt and Holly called in unison. "She's going to live!"

Mr. Acey came over to gaze down at the mare. "That's a good sign," he said, "but don't get your hopes up. The vet is on his way. He said he'd be here in about half an hour."

"Oh, my gosh," Matt called, remembering the time. He looked at the clock again. It was five fifteen. "I gotta go!"

"Me too!" Holly agreed.

"Will you let us know?" Matt asked Mr. Acey, and the fireman nodded.

Mr. Donald had leaned the bicycles against the firehouse wall. Now the pair hurried to ride them home.

Holly turned into her driveway, waving good-bye to Matt. Matt turned into the next driveway, coasting to a stop by the side of the house. He let out a shrill whistle. Almost immediately a neigh rang out and a brown-and-white pinto colt rushed up the fenceline to the tiny stable that sat beside the house.

"Hey, Patches!" Matt called. He threw his bike down and ran to give the colt a scratch. "Did you miss me, boy?"

Patches stretched his head across the fence rail, rubbing against Matt's sleeve affectionately. Then he began to sniff the sleeve and his top lip rolled back in a funny grimace.

"You smell the mare on my jacket, don't you,

boy?" He laughed as Patches continued to sniff the sleeve and then pawed the ground impatiently.

Matt scrubbed at the colt's neck with his fingertips, raising dirt to the surface, then stroking it away. "I have a lot to tell you, boy, but I gotta get inside first—before Mom kills me!"

Patches whinnied again as Matt hurried into the house.

"Mom!" Matt called as he came in the back door. "I'm home!"

"Well, it's about time," Matt's mom called back. She came into the kitchen then, rubbing her hands on a blue apron that hung from her neck and tied in the back. "I was beginning to worry."

"A lot happened."

"I should have known you'd be late." She went on. "You can't ever seem to drag yourself away from Assateague early enough to be on time for dinner." His mother's voice was weary but she smiled, so Matt knew she wasn't really upset.

"But, Mom, I have to tell you what happened."

Matt's mother stopped drying her hands and turned to listen. "You mean it isn't the usual, 'I found so many good pictures to shoot' story?"

"No!" he blurted out. "I only took a few pictures. That's because Holly and I found a mare half frozen in the freshwater pond near the Pony Loop! At first we thought she was dead, but she's not. She's in the firehouse and she's going to be okay. Can we go down there to check on her later this evening?"

"Whoa! Whoa! Slow down! You found a frozen pony and it was alive! So how did she get to the firehouse? I want to hear the whole story."

Matt took a deep breath and sat down. Then he told his mom everything that had happened. "So can we go down there later?" he asked again.

Mom shoved two plates of food into the microwave, pushed the buttons to reheat and sat down again. "You still have homework to do," she said. "How about if we call down there later on to see how she's doing? If she's still doing well, you can stop and check on her after school tomorrow. Okay?"

The microwave beeped and Mom pulled out the two steaming plates of dinner. "Okay?" she asked again.

Finally Matt nodded. "All right, but after we call to check on her, I'm going to call Danny and tell him everything. He's going to be sorry he didn't go with us today."

# four

"Hurry up, Danny!" Matt prodded his friend who was fumbling through a pile of messy papers in his desk. "Geez! How can you find anything in that mess?"

"Hey!" Danny said. "Can't you see I've got a system here? Just hold on a minute. I have to find that math worksheet Miss Baker told us to do tonight."

Matt shuffled his feet restlessly. "I want to see if Icy is up yet. Last night Mr. Donald said she was awake and trying to get up. The vet gave her medicine to make her sleep awhile longer. He said she needed the rest. But she should be up by now."

Danny threw a pile of papers back into his desk and stood up. His dark hair stood up in unruly spikes all over his head and his brown eyes danced mischievously.

"Just give me a few more minutes to find that worksheet," he mumbled. All at once a pile of books slid forward, tumbling out of Danny's desk. Matt looked at his friend and laughed. "Danny, you're a walking accident!"

Danny looked down. Then he began to laugh, too. "Hey, there's my math paper!" he yelled. He reached down to pick up the paper and his face split into a smile. "See! My system does work! Now, let's go see that Icy mare!"

Holly was waiting outside by the bike rack. The three of them got on their bikes and raced toward the firehouse. Holly grinned as she pulled into the fire-house first, followed closely by Matt. Danny was twenty feet back, jerking his handlebars in a zigzag pattern as he tried to hold onto the stack of papers in the bicycle's basket. The wind lifted one from the stack and sent it sailing behind him, but Danny didn't stop to pick it up. A second later he leaned his bike against the firehouse wall. He hopped off and looked at Holly and Matt. "Well? What are we waiting for?" he asked.

Inside the firehouse, the air was warm. Matt breathed in the smell of horse. One corner of the firehouse had been fixed up just for the pony. A wooden fence had been built to enclose the mare. Fresh yellow straw at least ten inches deep sur-rounded her, but she was still on her side.

Matt hurried forward. The mare turned her head to the side to see who was coming. As the three approached, Icy tried to stand, thrusting her front, legs out and pushing up, but the back legs crumpled weakly and she fell to her side again. Matt's heart sank.

Mr. Donald came up behind the three as they peered over the wooden fence. "She's really doing much better," he told them. His hand settled on Matt's shoulder. "The doctor said it will take a while for her to get her strength back. Her back legs were almost frozen, so we can only hope the blood begins to circulate properly again."

"She seems calm." Holly pushed her hair back as she spoke.

Mr. Donald released his grip on Matt's shoulder. "She seems to know we're helping her."

Matt slipped between the bars to kneel beside Icy. "Is it okay if we stay and talk to her awhile?"

"Sure." Mr. Donald smiled. "I think she would like that."

"Her name is Icy," Holly said.

"Oh yeah? And just how do you know that?" Mr. Donald asked.

"Matt told me."

Matt stroked the mare's face and neck. "I named her that yesterday."

"Oh, I see." Mr. Donald smiled as he turned to go back to the firehouse office. "Well, I'm counting on you to help me watch out for this little mare."

"I will!" Matt exclaimed.

"Me too!" Danny and Holly chimed in. "Mr. Donald," Matt called. The older man stopped. "Will you keep her here until she's better?"

"You betcha!"

On Friday, Matt had stopped to see the mare on his way home from school again. She was more lively, but that wasn't good. She wouldn't stop trying to get up. She was using all the energy that should have been helping her get well and the vet was worried. He said if she didn't stand soon, she might not ever. Her struggling was wasting her strength.

Matt thought about his visit as he groomed his own colt. Patches stood still as Matt massaged his body. The circular motions of the currycomb in his right hand pulled dirt and dust out of the pinto's coat. Matt used a brush in his left hand to brush it away. He worked silently, lost in thought.

If they could figure out a way to get Icy into a standing position, without putting her weight on the legs, maybe she would stop fighting. Maybe the blood would start to circulate. If they could prop her up somehow . . . maybe she would heal.

Patches turned his head to stare at his master. He grabbed the currycomb playfully between his teeth and tugged.

"Hey, you!" Matt tugged at the comb until Patches released his grip. "You aren't used to me being so quiet, are you, boy? You're used to me talking your ears off!" Matt thought a moment more. "Do you think you could help me figure something out? Can you tell me how to help the pinto mare?"

Patches shook his head from side to side, pawed the ground, then shook his head again.

"Okay! You're right," Matt agreed. "I *am* crazy!"

Matt pressed his head against the big brown patch on Patches's neck and breathed deeply. "I'm glad you're safe with me now," he told the colt.

Giving a final rub, Matt unhooked the lead shank from Patches's halter, turning the colt loose to run. But Patches didn't run. He followed Matt as the boy put away his grooming tools, filled the water tub and put a flake of hay in the manger. "See you in the morning," he told his colt as he closed the gate and headed for the house. He had to call the firehouse. He had to talk to Mr. Donald. He wanted to ask the fireman if propping the mare up would help. Maybe Mr. Acey and Mr. Donald could figure out a way to help Icy stand before her legs were ready.

# five

Saturday was clear and sunny and warmer than it had been in quite a while. Matt whistled as he pedaled his bike toward the firehouse. It was only nine o'clock in the morning, but the sky was as blue as the ocean in midsummer. Matt zoomed up the sidewalk and into the firehouse lot. Leaning his bike against the red brick building, he hurried inside.

Mr. Donald was on his knees in the center of the room. Matt glanced at Icy. She was still on her side and her eyes were glassy and sad. They followed him slowly as he crossed the room to stand by Mr. Donald.

"What are you doing?" Matt looked at the canvas strips by the fireman's feet. Mr. Donald looked like he was sewing the strips together.

"I'm taking you up on your idea, boy. We're going to make a pulley and get that mare to stand."

Matt knelt down, pushing his glasses back up on his nose.

"Hold these two pieces together for me, Matt."

While Matt held together two wide canvas strips, Mr. Donald worked a large curved needle with thread, up and down through the canvas, hooking the strips together, making them longer. Matt glanced at the strips at Mr. Donald's knees. Two had already been sewn together. Now a third was added.

"Canvas is about the strongest fabric you can

get," Mr. Donald told Matt. "I'm using nylon thread, too, because it can hold weight better, without breaking. We'll put these around the mare's belly, then use rope to pull her up."

Matt wasn't sure he understood, but he nodded anyway.

While Mr. Donald worked the needle in and out of the fabric, Matt watched Icy. She was calmer. She wasn't trying to stand like she had been the day before. Perhaps she had given up. Matt hoped not. She would need a strong will to survive.

Mr. Donald used his needle again, this time to attach two loops of leather, one to each end of the canvas belt.

"Okay. That should about do it," he said. Then he stood up and shook the long, wide strip of canvas out. "Want to help me put it on her?"

Matt nodded excitedly. He wanted to see how Mr. Donald's idea would work. Matt followed Mr. Donald to the corner where Icy was stretched out on her side, watching the two of them.

The firehouse door slammed. Matt turned to see. It was Mr. Acey, followed by Danny.

"I figured I'd find you here!" Danny said.

"Me too!" Mr. Acey added. "Hey, what are you two doing anyway?"

"Come over here," Mr. Donald instructed both of them. "You're just in time to help. We're going to get this mare up."

Then Mr. Donald got down on his knees next to Icy. "Help me pull this under her," he told Mr. Acey. Carefully the two worked the band under the mare, around her belly and up on the other side. Mr. Acey huffed and puffed as he lifted first one side of Icy and then the other.

Mr. Donald pulled the two loops together above her back. He wove a heavy rope through the loops, ran it under her belly, too, then back through the loops again. He knotted the ends together tightly.

Icy rolled her eyes and struggled. Then she

calmed. It was as if she knew they wanted to help her to stand.

Mr. Donald stood up. Then he threw the other end of the rope over a heavy metal ceiling beam. Matt and Danny watched as the rope sailed over the beam on the first try.

Mr. Donald pulled on the rope to test its strength. He looked at the others. "You ready to pull up this mare?"

No one spoke.

"Do you think we can do it?" Danny finally asked.

"Only one way to find out," Mr. Acey grabbed the rope and stood right next to Mr. Donald.

Matt took a deep breath and held the rope, too. Danny took hold of the end.

"You boys won't let go, will you?" Mr. Donald asked.

"No," they answered together.

"Then, on the count of three we pull. Okay?"

Danny and Matt nodded. Mr. Acey let go of the rope long enough to rub his hands on his pants. Then he grabbed it again.

"Let's do it, then," he said.

"One," Mr. Donald said slowly. He tugged the rope one more time and the knots held. "Two—three—"

Matt pulled the rope as hard as he could. He could feel Mr. Donald's muscles bulging against his side. Mr. Acey's face was red and strained. The rope began to slide across the beam, and slowly the mare started to rise.

Mr. Donald leaned back, carrying Matt with him. Danny was practically dangling on the end of the rope with all of his weight, adding to the pull.

"Keep pulling," Mr. Donald said.

The rope continued to slide across the beam and the mare inched upward . . . two feet . . . three feet . . .

All at once the mare was standing!

"Whoa!" Mr. Donald hollered. "Stop the rope, but don't let go."

Matt and Danny held the rope. They were hot and sweaty and red marks had been burned into the palms of their hands by the sliding rope. They watched as Mr. Donald tied the end of the rope to a hook on the side of the firehouse.

"You can let go now."

Matt watched the others release the rope. Then he let go, too. He rushed over to stand by the mare, to see if she was safe.

Icy was really standing now, with the help of the belly band and rope! Already she was moving around, seeing what she could reach. She lipped at the hay by her feet, then tried to take a step. The rope kept her in check. Danny grinned. She already seemed happier. She already seemed better!

"Well, I'll be a monkey's uncle," Mr. Acey said. He was grinning and rubbing his chin gently. "Who thought of this?"

Mr. Donald looked at Matt. "Wish I could say I did," he told his friend, "but it was Matt's idea."

Matt beamed with pleasure. Danny was scratching Icy's head and neck and the mare was leaning closer, wanting more. Maybe she would be all right after all!

# six

Holly hung on the fence, watching Matt lead his colt around the ring inside. Every now and then Patches would stop, plant his legs firmly and refuse to go. Then Matt would gently wrap his lead rope around the colt's rump and up again on the other side. After another tug, the colt would begin to walk again. Something about the pressure of the rope on his tail forced him to go.

"He almost knows how to lead now," Matt said. "If I keep working, he'll remember what he's supposed to do."

Holly climbed the fence to balance herself on the top rail. "I never knew you had to teach a pony to lead. I thought they just followed you naturally."

Matt led Patches over to the fence. "I wish it was that easy," he said. "When I first started breaking Patches to lead, I thought he would yank my shoulders off! Every time I'd tug the rope his eyes would roll and he'd back up. He hated it! Then Uncle Bob showed me how to wrap the rope around his back legs to urge him forward."

"It's hard to believe he would ever give you a hard time." Holly reached down to rub Patches on the swirl of hair under his forelock. "The way he follows you around . . . you can see he just adores you!"

Matt admired his colt a moment. "Do you think he remembers his mother or Assateague?"

Holly slipped down from the fence and leaned

into the colt, burying her face against his side. "I don't know," she answered slowly. "But I do know he's happy with you!"

"Matt!"

Matt turned to answer his mom. "Yeah?"

"Telephone! It's Mr. Donald!"

Matt felt his heart begin to thud in his chest. Mr. Donald had never called before! Was something wrong?

Holly slipped between the fence rails as Matt unhooked the lead rope. "Do you think it's about Icy?" she asked.

"I . . . I don't know," Matt stammered. He slid between the fence rails and hurried toward the house with Holly right on his heels.

He went in the door and Mom held the phone out to him.

Matt's chest tightened. "Is something wrong with Icy, Mr. Donald?" he asked without saying hello.

"Wrong? No, not a thing. In fact, I called with good news!"

Matt felt his shoulders relax. Holly was leaning close, her ear near the phone. Matt pushed her back. He put his hand over the mouthpiece. "It's okay," he told her. Then he listened as the fireman continued.

"That idea you had, boy . . . it was a good one! We just took the belly band and rope off. The mare is standing on her own now!"

Matt felt his face light up. "She's standing!"

"She's standing?" Holly squealed. "Icy is standing up all by herself?"

"Yes! Yes! Sshh!" Matt put his fingers to his lips, then spoke into the phone. "Is she okay?"

"She's just fine . . . standing here right now beside me, munching hay like she's the queen of the firehall. At first she was a little shaky, but she's great now. Just thought you should know, boy. After all, it was your idea."

Matt smiled. "Thanks," he said. "Thanks for letting me know!"

After he hung up, Matt told Holly the good news. Then he picked up the telephone to call Danny.

* * *

Matt sat on the step in front of his house and waited
for Danny. It was a gray, cold Saturday, but Danny
had said he would be on time today . . . ten A.M. Matt
looked at his watch. It was past ten. He rubbed his
foot back and forth over the fluffy white snow that
had frosted on the porch overnight. Two snows
already this year. That was a lot. It was a good thing
Icy wasn't still on Assateague.

As he waited, Matt tucked his camera under his
coat. The lump in the front of his shirt and coat
looked funny, but he didn't want to take a chance on
fogging the lens up. This was the first time he had
remembered to bring the camera since the day Icy
had been rescued.

Matt looked up. Danny was racing toward the
house, pedaling for all he was worth. His bicycle
slipped right, and then left, but somehow Danny
managed to keep it moving over the slippery spots
without falling. Just before he got to Matt, Danny
slammed on the brakes, sliding to a sideways stop

right in front of the step. The back wheel of the bike made a complete circle, leaving a doughnut-shaped impression in the inch of snow.

Danny dropped his bike and giggled. "Cool, huh?"

"Yeah, man, cool!" Matt couldn't help but grin back.

At the sound of voices, Patches wandered out of his stall, all sleepy-eyed, with his mane and tail full of loose straw. He stretched his head in the air and yawned, then walked tentatively through the snow.

"He looks like he's tiptoeing!" Danny said.

"It sort of does look like that," Matt agreed. "Hey, what do you think of this snow?"

"I can't believe it! We haven't had snow that really stuck for years. I was about five years old last time."

"No kidding!" Matt was amazed. "In Baltimore, we had snow on the ground every year. And Baltimore's not that far away."

Danny brushed the snow off his legs. "What do

you want to do today? Go see that pony again?"

"Do you mind if we go see how Icy is doing?" Matt asked.

"That sounds okay. I can ride my bike again. It's really fun in the snow!" The grin appeared on Danny's face again as he jumped on his bike and spun off, sliding sideways in the snow.

# seven

Matt slipped off a glove and reached into his pocket. He fingered the carrot he had brought as he walked toward the mare.

Icy stretched her head over the railing. Then she rumbled, soft and low, a nickery greeting that warmed Matt all the way to his frozen toes. Already she knew him! Already she was happy to see him!

He pulled the carrot from his pocket, snapping it into smaller pieces so she wouldn't choke. The crisp sound of it breaking induced another rumble from the mare. Icy's velvety soft lips sucked the carrot from Matt's palm. Strong white teeth crunched the pieces, then she reached out, lipping the hand, searching for more.

When the carrot was gone, she stood quietly, waiting for the scratching she knew she would get. She knew what to expect from Matt, and he wouldn't let her down.

Mr. Donald's deep bass voice didn't startle Matt today. He had known the fireman would be over to talk. From his office Mr. Donald could see all the comings and goings-on in the firehouse. On every visit, he came to greet Matt, and to give him a report on the mare's progress. "She's looking mighty fine, don't you think, Matt?"

"It's hard to believe she was so close to death just

a few weeks ago," Matt answered, nodding.

"Sure is, but she seems to be back to normal now. She's eating like a horse." Mr. Donald grinned. "Excuse the expression, but she is eating everything in sight! She moves around so much that we're thinking about fencing off a bigger area in here." He paused, then grinned again. "It's a good thing all the firemen like her. We haven't had a single complaint about letting a pony move in."

Matt watched the mare. As he rubbed her neck, her eyes closed and her head sunk lower, until she seemed to be near sleep. Of course the other firemen wouldn't protest, he thought. How could they? She was terrific.

Matt raised his camera from his neck and began to shoot pictures of the mare. Each time the flash popped the mare's eyes would jerk open, then they would drift shut again. As Matt snapped the pictures he began to worry. He took a deep breath. "When do you think you'll be taking her back to

Assateague Island?"

"We were discussing that just the other day . . .
me and the other firemen." Mr. Donald reached over
to rub the mare on the top of her mane. Matt could
tell Mr. Donald liked Icy, too. Icy opened her eyes
and reached up to nip Mr. Donald's coat gently.

Matt took another picture. "Have they decided
yet?"

"I think so. Most of us think we should wait until
spring."

Matt let out the breath he was holding.

"This winter has been harder than most island
winters. We don't want to take a chance . . ." Mr.
Donald got a thoughtful look on his face. "I still
can't figure out how she got stuck in that ice like
that." He patted the pony and turned to go back to
the office. "I guess that's one of those mysteries we'll
never figure out."

Danny walked up behind Matt. "How's she doing
today?" he asked.

"She's fine," answered Matt.

"She's getting fat!" Danny said.

Matt looked more closely at the mare. Danny was right! Already good food and lots of care were making the little mare fat.

# eight

"Matt! Holly is here!"

Matt heard his mom call from the front hall. He opened his bedroom door and hollered down the steps. "Send her up!" Then he got out the photographs he had just picked up yesterday from the pharmacy in town.

A moment later Holly appeared in the doorway. Her face was pale and she was carrying a wad of

Kleenex in her right hand.

"Still sick, huh?"

Holly nodded. "I still have this stupid cold, if that's what you mean. If it were up to my mom, she'd keep me inside forever! But Dad said to let me come over for a while. He said it would do me good to get out of the house."

"Just as long as you don't give it to me," Matt said.

"I won't," Holly promised. Then she saw the envelope in Matt's hand. "What've you got there?"

"My pictures of Icy," Matt said. "Want to see?"

Carefully, Matt spread the photos out on his bed. The first envelope contained pictures taken on the island before they had found Icy. It also had a picture of her taken on the firehouse floor that first day.

The second envelope held the pictures taken just the week before with Danny. Matt lined the photos up on the rumpled bedspread, in straight, neat lines.

"She's getting fat!" Holly said. "I can't believe

how fat she's getting!"

Matt studied the first picture he had taken of the mare. In it, her stomach was round too, but it was a bloated kind of round, not a healthy fat round. In the first picture, taken the day of her rescue, her shoulder bone jutted up and her hip bone stuck out. She was angular everywhere but in her stomach.

In the newer pictures, Icy was round all over. Her shoulders were filled out, thick and solid. Her hips were rounded and full. She looked healthy.

"See what good food and care can do?" Matt remarked.

Holly nodded, blew her nose, then looked at the pictures again.

In some of the pictures Icy was dozing on her feet. But in the last few she was alert, her ears up and her eyes curious. In the very last one she was gazing at Mr. Donald. It was the picture of a safe and healthy pony.

Matt gathered the photographs up, sliding them

back into the envelopes.

"I miss her," Holly said quietly. "I wish my mom would let me go see her today."

"Don't worry," Matt said. "Your cold will go away soon. But if it doesn't, I'll keep taking pictures to show you."

The winter was passing by quickly. Matt visited the mare almost every other day, sometimes with Danny, sometimes with Holly, but more often all alone. Icy whinnied at Matt every time he came. She munched on the treats he brought and rubbed against him lovingly. And she got fatter each day. The firemen were beginning to remark out loud about her weight, wondering if they were overfeeding her. But still they kept bringing her treats.

"Do you think she's getting too fat?" Matt asked Mr. Donald one day. "What if she is too fat? She might get sick again."

Mr. Donald laughed. "No, son," he told Matt. "I

think she is just the right weight for her condition."

On the way home Matt wondered what he could possibly mean when he said "her condition"? Her condition was good—wasn't it?

# nine

Matt brushed the dried mud from Patches's coat with short brisk strokes. It had dried and caked over the past few days. Every now and then Patches would jerk away from the brush. He didn't like the pulling feeling when the mud finally released its hold on his coat. Along with the mud, big handfuls of Patches's winter coat came out. Matt whistled as he worked, enjoying the warm day, his pony and the chore.

Finally winter was breaking its hold on the island. There hadn't been any more snow, but the ocean breezes had been cold and the ground had been frozen for a long time. Then the ground had thawed. Now the warm breezes were drying up the mud holes in Patches's pasture.

Matt began to work on the pony's mane, using the metal comb. He pulled the tangles away and smoothed the hair down. It had grown since fall. It was getting thick and coarse and losing its coltlike softness.

Patches lifted his nose and sniffed the air. He tossed his head playfully. Even the young pony could feel the scent of spring blowing on the warm air.

Soon it would be time to return Icy to Assateague. Matt was surprised the firemen hadn't returned her by now, but he wasn't complaining. He loved visiting her, watching her and being with her.

"Hey, Matt, what are you doing?"

Matt jumped at the sound of Holly's voice.

"Just cleaning up Patches."

"Want to ride down to the firehouse with me to see Icy?"

Matt began to put the grooming tools into the big bucket by his feet. "Sounds good to me!"

He was getting his bicycle from the garage when his mom came out. "Telephone for you," she said. "It's Mr. Acey."

Matt stepped inside and took the receiver from his mom's hand. "Hello?"

He leaned his ear into the phone as Mr. Acey spoke.

"I think you'd better come down here," Mr. Acey said softly.

Matt waited for a reason. When none came he asked, "Is something wrong?"

"Sakes, no!" Mr. Acey replied. "There's just something here I think you should see! Now don't go asking me what," the fireman added. "Just get on down here as soon as you can."

Holly and Matt pedaled their bikes as fast as they

could down Main Street toward the firehouse. Matt's mind raced as fast as the wheels on his bike.

Maybe Icy was sick. She was definitely too fat. No, Mr. Acey had said nothing was wrong. Then why had Mr. Acey called?

In front of the firehouse, Matt skidded to a stop. He leaned his bike against the firehouse wall. Holly came streaming in behind him, then let her bike crash to the ground. Together they raced inside.

Across the room a crowd had gathered around Icy's pen. Matt dashed across the room. "What's wrong?" he cried.

Mr. Donald and Mr. Acey turned to grin at him.

"Nothing's wrong!" Mr. Donald answered. "Just see for yourself."

The fireman let Matt and Holly in front of him so they could see.

"Oh!" Holly gasped.

Matt looked in wonder at Icy. She was lying on her side. Stretched out beside her was a brand-new, shiny, wet foal. He was coal-black, without a sliver of white to be found. With the firehouse lights shining down, a hint of royal purple glinted on the coat.

"He's really something, isn't he?" Mr. Acey asked.

"Yes," Matt said, and beside him Holly nodded.

Icy scrubbed her new colt with her tongue, then looked up at Matt. She stretched her neck toward him and he touched her velvet nose. "You did good," he murmured.

"She sure did," Mr. Donald agreed.

"She wasn't really fat, was she?" Matt asked. He felt numb all over.

"No, Matt. She wasn't fat!"

Matt watched the two lying close and he closed his eyes, remembering that day on Assateague . . . remembering when Patches was born.

"We're expecting you to give this little fellow a name," Mr. Donald added.

"Me? Really?"

"Sure! There wasn't any one of us as dedicated as you have been to this mare. You deserve to name her colt before we set them free again."

Holly tugged on Mr. Donald's sleeve. "When will that be?" she asked. "When will you turn her loose?"

"We'll give the colt a few weeks to get his strength. Then it would be best to let them go. They need to find their herd."

Matt slipped carefully between the rails. But he needn't have worried. The once-wild mare knew and trusted him. Kneeling beside the two, Matt whispered a greeting to the new colt.

# *ten*

"You coax her into the trailer, Matt. She trusts you."

Matt walked up the ramp and into the trailer, the red bucket of oats he'd brought from home swinging on his arm. He hoped it would work. He didn't want to let Mr. Donald down.

"Come on, Icy," he called softly. He swished the oats around in the bucket, then took a handful and held it up. He let the oats slip between his fingers so Icy could see and hear them.

Icy's ears came up. She snorted then turned to look at her colt. The colt bumped against her back legs gently with his head, rubbing playfully, then jumping to one side.

"Come on, girl. See the oats? Come and get them."

Icy snorted again, then took a cautious step. The trailer ramp creaked loudly and Matt grimaced. But the mare didn't flinch as he had expected. Instead she took another step.

Matt stretched out his hand, spilling oats on the ramp in front of her. The mare lipped up the oats and took another step. Slowly she followed the trail of grain up the ramp and into the back of the trailer. The colt cowered behind, stepping forward in time with his mother.

As soon as she was in the trailer, Mr. Donald eased the ramp up and closed the back. Matt slid out the front with a grin on his face.

"That was a lot easier than I thought it would

be," Mr. Donald said. He was smiling, too, and so was Mr. Acey. Holly leaned against the back of the trailer and peered inside.

"What are they doing?" Matt asked.

"Ssshh!" Holly held her fingers up to her lips. "The colt's nursing."

"Well, they can't get more relaxed than that!" Mr. Acey chuckled. "I guess it's time to get this pair back home."

"Let's take those last two bales of hay along," Mr. Donald suggested. "We might as well put them out for the ponies. We don't have any use for them now."

Something about the way Mr. Donald spoke gave Matt an empty feeling. No use for them now . . . it echoed in his mind. Matt tagged along behind the older fireman, into the firehouse.

Over in the corner, part of the railing had been taken down to bring Icy and the foal out. The straw was scattered on the floor. The railing hung in a broken section. It seemed so empty now.

Without speaking, Matt and Mr. Donald stacked

the two bales of hay on top of each other and dragged them out to the trailer. Mr. Donald picked them up and put them in the back of the pickup truck.

"Okay, let's get going." Mr. Donald brushed the hay from his pants and slid into the driver's side of the truck.

"Come on, kids!" Mr. Acey slid in on the passenger side and Holly and Matt jumped in beside him. The truck ground to a start and began rolling, pulling the trailer effortlessly behind.

They crossed the bridge onto Assateague Island. Matt watched the herons rising from the bay. He rolled the window down a little and breathed in the warm March air. He felt funny . . . glad to be returning the mare, yet sad, too.

"Did you think of a name for that colt yet, boy?" Mr. Donald asked.

"Sort of."

"What's that mean, sort of? Either you did or you didn't."

"I thought, well, maybe, Icicle," Matt said softly.

"Did he say Icicle?"

"Yes."

"Well, I think that's a fine name!" Mr. Acey boomed.

"It's perfect!" Holly laughed. "Little Icicle—the son of Icy. It's perfect!"

Matt smiled. "His color reminded me of the icicles I saw hanging from my bedroom window in the winter. At night, when the lights hit them they were dark, reflecting colors . . . just like the colt."

"That's neat!" Holly poked Matt with her elbow and he shoved her back.

Mr. Donald drove past the ranger station and past the trail that led up to the lighthouse. He pulled off the road near the sign that said Pony Loop.

As soon as Mr. Donald lowered the ramp, Icy trotted right out of the trailer. Little Icicle walked down cautiously, then jumped the last two feet, landing beside his mother with a startled look.

Icy stood still while Mr. Acey tossed the bales of hay from the truck. Icicle huddled beside her. It was as if they didn't know they were free.

Matt reached out to rub the mare's neck and she leaned into him. Icicle peered around her legs, sniffing Matt's pant legs and snorting playfully.

"I loved getting to know you," Matt told the mare. "I'm going to miss coming to see you," he added.

"Me too!" Holly was rubbing the mare on top of her head.

All at once the mare's head shot up and she snorted. A neigh rang out.

Matt stepped backward. Every nerve in his body jumped as a black stallion suddenly appeared, pawing and snorting.

Holly and Matt moved behind the truck with Mr. Donald and Mr. Acey. They watched as the stallion came for his mare.

First they touched noses, then snorted again. The black stallion pushed the tiny colt out of his way as he circled the mare, sniffing and pushing. When he had decided that this was indeed his own missing mare, he shoved her again, only harder. He sent his bugle up like an order, a whinny that sliced through the air like a knife.

The stallion pranced forward, commanding Icy to follow, and the mare did as she was told. Icicle mimicked the stallion, prancing along behind his mother. Icy looked back once and it seemed to Matt as if her eyes met his.

Matt felt as if he was alone. The air around him still smelled of Icy and her foal. If he closed his eyes maybe she would be there, with him, again.

Matt leaned against the trailer and shut his eyes. He pictured Icy frozen in the pond. Matt opened his eyes to watch Icy follow the black stallion and felt warm all over. It was good that Icy was going home, back to the herd of her birth. It was because of them, Matt thought. They had saved her and they had brought Icy home again.

*Lois Szymanski* lives in Westminster, Maryland, with her husband, Dan, her Shetland Sheepdog named Ryley, and three cats. She and her oldest daughter have two horses—one of them a Chincoteague pony named Sea Feather. When Lois isn't writing, she stays busy doing agility training with her dog, talking to students, and dreaming up new stories about horses. You can visit Lois Szymanski online at www.loisszymanski.com.

# CHARMING PONIES

CHARMING PONIES
## A Perfect Pony

Will Nicki choose the pony of her...

CHARMING PONIES
## A Pony Promise
...ny needs a mother's love, too.

**Each book includes a unique charm. COLLECT THEM ALL!**

CHARMING PONIES
## A Pony to the Rescue

Could a spooky old legend actually be *true*?

CHARMING PONIES
## A Pony to Remember

Will Jenny ever see her pony again?

HarperFestival®
*A Division of HarperCollins*Publishers

www.harpercollinschildrens.com